The GREAT EXPLORER

CHRIS
JUDGE

ANDERSEN PRESS

For Mum and Dad

First published in Great Britain in 2012 by Andersen Press Ltd., 20 Vauxhall Bridge Road, London SW1V 2SA.
Published in Australia by Random House Australia Pty., Level 3, 100 Pacific Highway, North Sydney, NSW 2060.
Text and illustration copyright © Chris Judge, 2012. The rights of Chris Judge to be identified as the author and illustrator of this work have been asserted by him in accordance with the Copyright, Designs and Patents Act, 1988. All rights reserved. Printed and bound in Singapore by Tien Wah Press. British Library Cataloguing in Publication Data available. ISBN 978 1 84939 401 7

10   9   8   7   6   5   4   3   2

Tom's dad was a famous explorer.

One morning when Tom went down to breakfast . . .

THE NEWS

he was shocked to see a picture of his dad
on the front of the morning paper.

His dad had got lost while
exploring the North Pole.

Tom resolved there and
then to go and rescue him.

First, he studied his globe of the world and found the North Pole.

Then he bought a map so he could
find his way there . . .

packed his bag and set off on his first adventure.

Saucepan

Tent

Compass

Matches

Sleeping bag

Cup

Flares

Pick

Fishing Rod

Torch

Food

Binoculars

Casting off, he set sail
out into the big, blue ocean.

After sailing for many weeks, Tom knew he was close to the North Pole when gigantic icebergs appeared on the horizon.

As he sailed on, he saw lots of beautiful shapes in the ice.

It was the most magical place he had ever seen.

But soon the ice got thicker and thicker . . .

until eventually the boat ran aground on the ice!

Fortunately Tom had a hot air balloon on board.

He pumped it full   of hot air . . .

and soon it was ready to take off.

He unhitched the rope and up it went!

As night fell, the spectacular Northern Lights lit up the sky.

Tom was amazed.

But the balloon sailed too high and was hit by a passing satellite!

The balloon plummeted downwards.

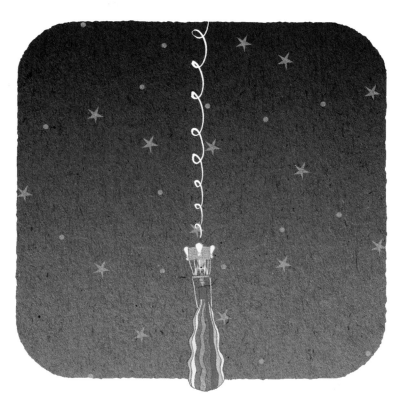

"AAAAAHHH!"

Tom screamed with fright.

Luckily he had a
parachute with him.

Quickly he put it on
and jumped out.

"Phew! That was a close shave!" he thought,
as the balloon crashed to the ground.

But just at that
moment . . .

he landed on top of a very dangerous cliff.

Undaunted, he sat on his coil of rope and slid . . .

all the way down.

But just as he reached the bottom he skidded into . . .

Tom ran away as fast as he could until he reached a dangerous river of broken ice.

So he jumped . . .

hopped . . .

skipped . . .

bounded . . .

and leapt

across the ice until he was safely on the other side.

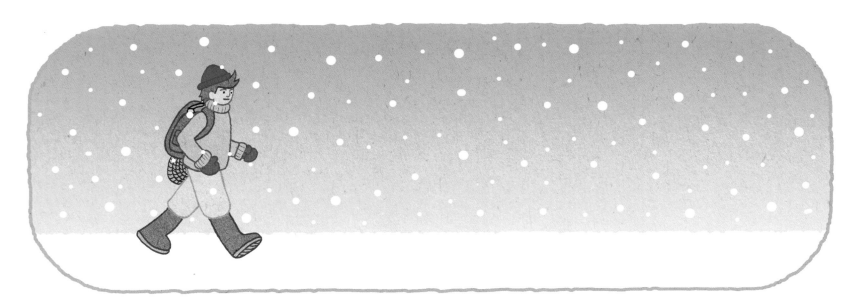

As Tom continued his journey, it started to snow heavily.

The blizzard grew wilder still, so he decided to pitch his tent.

But the wind was too strong and his tent blew away!

Fortunately he spotted a small cave.

He crept inside and

was just settling down to have a rest when . . .

Tom ran away as fast as he could.

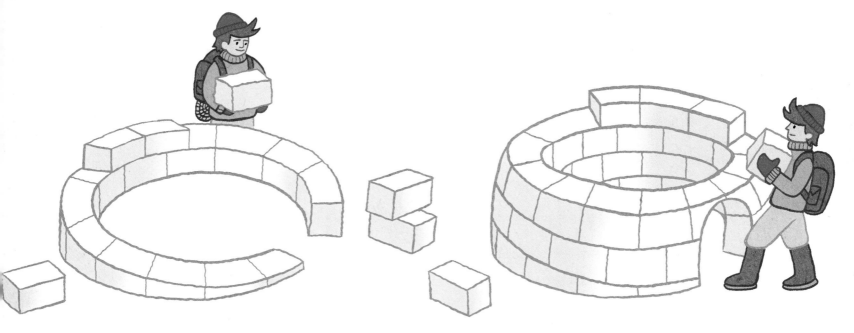

It was getting dark so he decided to build
an igloo to shelter in.

He built a fire to cook his dinner and laid out his sleeping bag for the night.

Tom rose early the next morning to find it had stopped snowing.

He dug a hole in the ice to catch some fish for breakfast before setting out for the day.

Finally, just as the sun was setting, Tom spotted a familiar tent on the horizon.

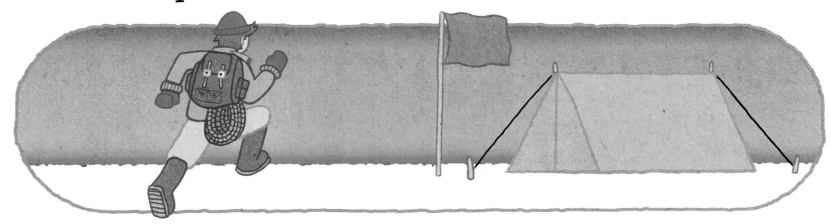

"Dad!" he shouted, as he ran as fast as he could towards it.

His dad was so happy
to see him.

He had broken his foot when he fell from a cliff,

and had been unable to let his rescuers know where he was.

Tom took a flare from his bag and signalled for help.

Luckily it was spotted by a rescue helicopter that was in the area and they were soon hoisted to safety.

As they headed for home, Tom told his dad about the great adventures that he'd had on the way to rescue him.

"We will call *you* The Great Explorer from now on," said his dad proudly when they were safely home. "I wonder where our next adventure will take us?"